Lindsey: 964-6599

Amanda: 254-1308

Jim Henson's Muppet Stories™

Starring Jim Henson's Muppets™

Jim Henson's Muppet Stories

Produced by Jim Henson Productions
in conjunction with Funk & Wagnalls Corporation
Distributed by Funk & Wagnalls Corporation

★

JIM HENSON PRODUCTIONS

Jane Leventhal
Publisher

Ellen Weiss
Senior Project Editor

Louise Gikow
Editorial Director

Lauren Attinello
Art Director

Laura Hawk
Marketing Director

★

FUNK & WAGNALLS

Edward Volkwein
Publisher

Scott Iacone
Associate Publisher

James Wagenvoord
Editor at Large

Patricia Coen
Senior Editor

Kate Davis
Associate Editor

Michele Italiano-Perla
Executive Art Director

Murray Keshner
Art Director

Maggie Peterson
Assistant Art Director

Christopher Moffa
Marketing Associate

Kermit's All-Time
Favorites

Hi-ho! Kermit the Frog here. You know, friends come in all shapes and sizes. They don't have to look the same or act the same . . . or even be the same.

That's what the Fraggles learn in one of my favorite stories, "The Round Number Ticker." Now, you might think that a Round Number Ticker—that's a watch to us Silly Creatures—is a pretty silly friend. But the Fraggles realize that anything—no matter how strange—can be a true friend in a time of trouble.

Benny the Bluebird has some unusual friends, too, in "Forever Green." They are the fir trees, who shelter him from the cold during a very stormy winter. Did you ever think a tree could be your friend? Well, maybe trees aren't the same kinds of friends as boys and girls are. But trees give us a lot, like shade from the sun and great places to climb. That seems pretty friendly to me. Look around you. The world is full of friends!

Sincerely,

Kermit

Table of Contents

Kermit's Lullaby

"Settle down, Robin," Kermit said. "It's time to go to sleep."

"But, Uncle Kermit," Robin answered, sitting up in bed, "I don't feel sleepy at all!"

"Try counting salamanders," Kermit said, sitting down beside Robin.

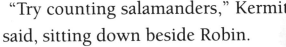

By Richard Chevat

Illustrated by Richard Walz

"I tried that," Robin complained. "It didn't work."

"Well, what might work?" Kermit wanted to know.

"Sing me a lullaby," Robin answered.

"Okay," Kermit said. "But just one. And then, off to sleep! Now, lie down and close your eyes."

"Yes, Uncle Kermit," said Robin, and Kermit began to sing softly:

> *"Hush, little tadpole,*
> *don't make a croak,*
> *Momma's gonna . . ."*

"That's not how it goes," said Robin. "It's 'Hush, little baby, don't say a word.'"

"This is the frog version," said Kermit. "Now, listen." And he began again:

> *"Hush, little tadpole, don't make a croak,*
> *Momma's gonna buy you a place to soak.*
> *And if that place to soak springs a leak,*
> *Momma's gonna buy you a house in the creek."*

"In the creek?" Robin said, sitting up. He tried to imagine what a house in a creek looked like. "Why does he want a house in a creek?"

"Because tadpoles like creeks!" Kermit replied. "Now, hush!"

"Okay," said Robin. "But it sounds funny."

"Lie down!" said Kermit, and he started singing once more:

> *"And if that house in the creek should break,*
> *Momma's gonna buy you a muddy lake.*
> *And if that muddy lake goes dry . . ."*

"Uncle Kermit?" Robin interrupted.

"Yes?" said Kermit.

"Why does the lake go dry?"

"Why?" Kermit sighed. "Just because!"

"Oh," Robin said.

"Where was I?" Kermit asked.

"The lake went dry," answered Robin.

"Oh, yeah," said Kermit. And he sang:

> *"And if that muddy lake goes dry,*
> *Momma's gonna buy you a dragonfly.*
> *And if that dragonfly . . ."*

"Uncle Kermit?"

"Yes?" groaned Kermit.

"Why do they call it a dragonfly?"

"Why, why, why?" Kermit cried. "Because! Now, don't ask me why anymore!"

"Why?" asked Robin.

"Robin, do you want me to sing this song or not?" Kermit asked.

"Yes, please, Uncle Kermit," said Robin.

"Then please don't interrupt me anymore!" Kermit begged.

And he started the song all over again from the beginning:

> *"Hush, little tadpole, don't make a croak,*
> *Momma's gonna buy you a place to soak.*
> *And if that place to soak springs a leak,*
> *Momma's gonna buy you a house in the creek.*
> *And if that house in the creek should break,*
> *Momma's gonna buy you a muddy lake.*
> *And if that muddy lake goes dry,*

Momma's gonna buy you a dragonfly.
And if that dragonfly is bad,
Momma's gonna buy you a lily pad.
And if that lily pad gets soggy,
Momma's gonna buy you a swamp that's boggy.
And if that swamp stops being a bog,
Momma's gonna buy you a hollow log.
And if that log turns upside down,
you'll still be the cutest little tadpole around."

Kermit sang the whole song, and when he was done, Robin didn't say a thing. His head was on the pillow and his eyes were closed.

"Asleep at last," Kermit said softly.

He stood up and began to tiptoe out of the room.

Just as he reached the door, he heard a little frog voice. It was Robin's.

"That was nice, Uncle Kermit," he said. "Sing it again."

"Oh, why?" Kermit sighed.

"Because," mumbled Robin, and then he nodded off to sleep.

Sweet Dreams

Here's a nice lullaby to sing at bedtime with someone you love. Point to each picture on the right as you sing along.

Rock-a-bye

In the  top.

When the wind blows,

The  will rock.

When the bough breaks,

The  will fall.

And down will come

 and all.

The Garage Sale

Every spring, Miss Piggy cleaned up her house from top to bottom. Every spring, she washed windows, aired out pillows, and beat rugs. And every spring, she noticed that she had more and more things to clean.

One year, it just got to be too much.

By Harry Ross

Illustrated by Richard Walz

"This house is too crowded," she said to herself. "I think I'll throw out some of this old junk I never use."

She was just about to get out the jumbo garbage bags when she had an idea.

"I'll have a garage sale!" she said.

She went to the store and got some tagboard and a hot pink marker and made a sign. It said:

CObe One! Come All!
Garage Sale Tomorrow!
Great Stuff!

She posted the sign on her front lawn and then gathered together the things she wanted to get rid of.

There was her pink bowling ball from the Piggyback League.
There were her sugarplum fairy wings from the costume ball.
There were some ski boots that rubbed and some sandals that squeaked and an old kitty cat clock that went *tock tick* instead of *tick tock*.
There was a box of old books and beauty magazines.

Bright and early the next day, she brought everything out to her garage.

Kermit was the first to come. "Interesting clock," he said.

Piggy looked at the kitty cat clock and remembered the Christmas morning she had found it beneath her tree. It *was* cute.

"It says *tock tick* instead of *tick tock*," she pointed out.

"I still like it," said Kermit.

"So do I," said Piggy. "I'm sorry, Kermie, I've changed my mind. It's not for sale."

"Okay," said Kermit. He moved on to look at something else.

Then Gonzo showed up.

"Hey, these wings are really nifty," he said, trying them on.

When she saw them on Gonzo, Piggy remembered the costume ball and how ravishing she had looked.

"They *are* nifty," she agreed. "I'm sorry, Gonzo. They're not for sale. Besides, they don't do a thing for you."

Fozzie was fiddling with the boots, Rowlf was rummaging through the old books, and Animal was trying to jam the squeaky sandals onto his feet.

Suddenly, Piggy could not stand it for one more second.

"Hold everything!" she yelled, so loudly that Kermit dropped the bowling ball half an inch from his toe.

"I've changed my mind," continued Piggy in a very small voice. "I'm sorry, but the garage sale is off."

Everyone stood still, amazed.

"Just because I don't use these things anymore," explained Piggy, "it doesn't mean I don't need them. They bring back wonderful memories. Each one of these is a part of me. These things are really special to me . . . and I want to keep them. Please forgive me, everyone."

"We understand," said Kermit, smiling.

"Sure we do," said Gonzo. "But there is one thing I'd still really like to buy."

"Gonzo, whatever it is, it's not for sale," said Piggy in exasperation.

"I'll bet it is," said Gonzo. "I really want to buy that nice garage sale sign, Piggy. You see, I have a lot of great stuff I don't need anymore, and—"

"No, Gonzo," laughed Piggy. "It's still not for sale." She began gathering up her beloved things to take inside. "It's free. You can have it!"

Far-Out Talent

It was almost show time at the Muppet Theater. The singing chickens were warming up, the juggling hippos were practicing, and Fozzie Bear was trying out his new jokes.

"Kermit! Kermit! Hold everything!" Scooter came running in, looking very excited.

By Richard Chevat

Illustrated by Richard Walz

"What's wrong?" Kermit asked impatiently. "Did the penguins forget their bow ties again?"

"No, no!" Scooter cried. "Creatures from outer space have landed!"

"Creatures from outer space!" Kermit said nervously. "Are they here to invade earth?"

"I don't think so," said Scooter. "They look pretty friendly."

Everyone gathered around as a group of six strange-looking space creatures appeared backstage.

No one had ever seen anything like them. They each had three arms, five green eyes, and bright orange fur. But strangest of all were the small propellers on the tops of their heads.

One of the space creatures stepped forward. The propeller on his head started to spin, and soon he was floating a few inches off the floor.

"Hello, green creature," the floating space visitor said to Kermit.

"Kermit!" said Gonzo excitedly. "They're great! Maybe we could put them in the show!"

Kermit thought for a few seconds.

"Gee, I don't know," he said, turning to the aliens. "Do you guys have an act?"

"What is an ax?" the creature asked in its weird voice.

"You know," explained Kermit, "something to do onstage. Do you dance?"

"Dunce? What is dunce?" asked the space being as he slowly flew around Kermit.

"Hey, I have an idea!" Gonzo said. "You can sing with the singing chickens!"

"Zing? We no zing," all the aliens said sadly. Then **they too** rose up into the air.

"Maybe they play music," suggested Rowlf.

"No musics," they replied, while they floated around the room.

"How about telling jokes?" said Fozzie. "Did you hear the one about the two Martians? They wanted to stay overnight on the moon, but they couldn't because the moon was full. Get it? A full moon! Wocka, wocka!"

"Hmmm, jukes. No, we know no jukes," said the first creature.

He was so sad that his teeth almost touched the ground.

"I'm sorry," said Kermit. "But you don't dance, sing, play music, or tell jokes. I just don't know what you could do in the show."

"We no have ax," the alien agreed. "We go home."

And slowly they flew out the door.

"Gee, too bad," said Gonzo. "They seemed like nice space creatures."

"Yeah," Fozzie nodded. "I wish they did something besides fly around all the time."

"Yeah," added Kermit. "'They sure did fly a lot."

Then suddenly he had an idea.

"Hey! They can fly! That would be a great act! Scooter, go catch them, quick!"

Soon the space creatures were onstage, flying around and doing flips and rolls in the air.

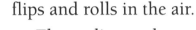

The audience cheered and applauded.

"You guys can perform here every night," Kermit said to them after the show.

"No, thanks," said the aliens' leader. "We must go now."

"But why?" asked Kermit. "You were great!"

"No can stay," explained the creature as he floated to the door. "Must return to our planet with valuable discovery—jukes! Did you hear the one about the two Martians?"

"Good-bye!" everyone shouted as the spaceship took off and flew away.

"Come back soon!" called Kermit. We really loved your ax!"

Baby Gonzo Gets His Wish

By Ellen Weiss

Illustrated by Tom Cooke

"Hey, look at this!" exclaimed Gonzo. He'd been banging and clanking around the very back of the kitchen closet, while Nanny washed the dishes from lunch.

"What did you find, Gonzo?" asked Nanny.

"I don't know, but it's neat," said Gonzo. "I think it might be a gold nose-cover."

Nanny turned to look, and then she laughed.

"Oh, that's an old brass lamp," she said. "It's been in the back of the closet for so long, it's all tarnished. Would you like to polish it?"

"Sure!" said Gonzo.

So Nanny gave him some polish and a cloth, and he sat down in a corner and started to work. He rubbed and he rubbed, and the lamp got shinier and shinier. And as he rubbed, he began to daydream.

Suddenly, a wisp of blue smoke began snaking out of the lamp—and then a whole cloud of smoke. And out of the smoke stepped a strange-looking fellow with a large mustache.

"I am the genie of the lamp," announced the fellow. "Thank you for letting me out. What are your three wishes?"

"You mean, I can just wish for something and you'll arrange it?" asked Gonzo in amazement.

"Your wish is my command," said the genie.

"Okay," said Gonzo, thinking hard. "This is great! I'll have all the marshmallows in the world, please."

The genie nodded. All at once, Gonzo heard a loud roaring sound and began to smell the sweet smell of marshmallows in the air. And then they started coming . . . millions of marshmallows . . . billions of marshmallows . . . pouring in the windows . . . knocking down the doors . . . even coming out of the kitchen faucet. They filled up the kitchen, piling up higher and higher, until they were up to Gonzo's nose. In a minute, he was going to be covered in marshmallows!

"Wait!" yelled Gonzo, his voice muffled by marshmallows. "Hold on! Cancel that wish! Forget it! Ixnay on the wish!"

"Your wish is my command," said the genie, and the marshmallows disappeared.

"Whew! That was close!" gasped Gonzo. "I'll have to be more careful with the next wish."

Gonzo began thinking. He thought and he thought, until the genie began to tap his foot. But at last, Gonzo had it.

"I wish I could fly," he said.

"No problem," said the genie.

Gonzo gave his arms a little test flap, just to see what would happen. He rose into the air about a foot. Flapping harder, he shot up into the air and bumped into the kitchen ceiling.

"Ow!" he said. He rubbed his head, flapped his arms sideways, and sailed straight through the kitchen window.

Unfortunately, he'd forgotten about the sycamore tree that was just outside the window.

"Ooch!" he said, rubbing his nose where it had hit the tree. He flew back into the kitchen.

Gonzo's arms were getting very tired. "I think it's time to take a rest," said Gonzo to himself, flapping toward the floor. But, as hard as he tried, he couldn't seem to land. He just floated about in the middle of the room.

"Hey, Mr. Genie!" called Gonzo. "Why can't I land?"

"You didn't wish anything about landing," said the genie. "Only flying."

"Let me down, you meanie-genie!" said Gonzo.

"Okay, I'll do you a favor. But just this once," said the genie. He let Gonzo down with a loud thump.

"I wish you were never in that lamp!" cried Gonzo, rubbing his knee.

And in that instant, Gonzo wasn't rubbing his knee anymore. He was rubbing the lamp.

"Good job!" said Nanny. "It's nice and shiny."

Gonzo peered inside the lamp. "And it's nice and empty, too," he added. "Thank goodness."

19

Forever Green

By Michaela Muntean
Illustrated by John Gurney

One summer, many summers ago, a bluebird named Benny fell out of his nest and broke his wing.

Summer slowly turned to fall; there was a coolness in the air, and the days were growing shorter. The robins felt it, and so did the cardinals and the wrens and all the other birds.

Benny felt it, too. It was time to begin flying south for the winter, but Benny's wing still had not healed. He would never be able to make the long trip.

The other birds tidied their nests and promised to meet again in the spring.

As they flew away, Benny sadly waved good-bye to all his friends. He had never spent the winter in the North, but he knew that he would need a safe, warm place to stay until spring arrived.

Benny asked a birch tree if he could live in its branches for the winter.

"Oh, no," said the birch tree. "I have enough to do just to take care of myself without taking care of the likes of you. Go away, little bird."

Next, Benny asked a big oak tree if he might spend the winter in the warmth of its branches.

"How do I know you won't eat my acorns?" said the big oak tree.

"I promise I won't," said Benny.

"I don't believe you," said the oak tree. "I've never trusted bluebirds and I'm not about to start now. Go away, little bird."

So Benny sadly went to the next tree he saw, which was a tall willow.

"Oh, willow tree," said Benny, "may I please spend the winter in your long, beautiful branches?"

But the willow tree just shook its head and said, "I'm trying to take a nap. Go away, little bird, and don't bother me!"

A pine tree, standing nearby, overheard what the willow tree had said.

"Come here, little bluebird," said the pine tree. "I have many warm branches; you may stay with me until spring arrives."

"Oh, thank you," said Benny, and he happily hopped up into the pine tree's branches.

A spruce tree had also been listening all this time and said, "I will protect you and the pine tree from the strong northern winds. Don't worry, little bluebird. You will be safe and warm until springtime."

A little juniper tree had been listening as well, and it said, "I will have berries all winter, and I have plenty to spare, so you will not go hungry."

And as Benny settled gratefully into his new home, winter arrived in the forest.

The snow swirled, the wind howled, and riding on the wind was the great Jack Frost himself.

"I have heard," said Jack Frost, "about the selfishness of *some* trees in this forest. I have also heard of the kindness of others. Therefore, this winter—and all winters ever after," he decreed, "all trees will lose their leaves and stand bare and cold until spring arrives. All trees, that is, except for the pine and spruce and juniper, which will remain forever green."

The bluebird made it through the winter just fine.

And the pine, the spruce, and the juniper? They stayed as green as ever, all winter long—and they still do.

The Round Number Ticker

Gobo's Uncle Traveling Matt had left Fraggle Rock a long time ago to see the wide world. He spent most of his days studying the puzzling ways of those he called the "Silly Creatures" (we call them "people").

By Deborah Kovacs

Illustrated by Larry DiFiori

One day, Gobo received a package from Traveling Matt. Inside was a round, flat something. The thing had these numbers on it: 1 2 3 4 5 6 7 8 9 10 11 12, all in a circle. It had three sticks on it of different sizes, which pointed at the numbers. Strangest of all, it made a sound like this: *tick-tick-tick-tick*.

There was also a letter in the package, which said:

"Dear Nephew:
Here is your very own Round Number Ticker. Silly Creatures wear these things on their arms and look at them all day long. Sometimes these things make the most shocking buzzing, ticking, and beeping sounds. I think they are trying to make friends with their owners. But the Silly Creatures never answer them. I hope you can make friends with this Round Number Ticker.

With love,
Uncle Traveling Matt."

Gobo didn't know what to do with his present. But he wanted to be friendly. "Hello," he said to it.

Tick-tick-tick-tick, answered the Round Number Ticker.

"Hmmm," said Gobo. "Maybe you don't speak Fragglish. I'll talk to you in your language."

So he said, "Tick-tick-tick-tick."

Tick-tick-tick-tick, answered the Round Number Ticker.

"We're getting somewhere . . . I guess," said Gobo. "But I hope I can teach you some new things to say."

Gobo tried to get the Round Number Ticker to say new things.

He sang it Fraggle songs, like "I'll Make You a Radish Pie as Big as Your Head."

He told it stories, like "Why Fraggles Do Somersaults Every Day."

He took it on a hike to the Farthest Cave.

But it never learned any new words.

After a while, the Fraggles still hadn't gotten anywhere with the Round Number Ticker.

"It's been here for days, and it still hasn't learned a word of Fragglish," said Red.

"Maybe we should find out if it likes to swim," said Gobo.

He took it into the Great Pool with him and then let it go.

The Round Number Ticker sank slowly to the bottom. But even from the bottom of the Great Pool, the Fraggles still could hear the Round Number Ticker saying the same thing it always did: *tick-tick-tick-tick*.

"Maybe it's happy down there," said Red.

Soon the Fraggles forgot about the Round Number Ticker. But later that day, they were picnicking at the Great Pool, at just the spot where Gobo had thrown his present into the water. Suddenly, the Round Number Ticker said something totally new. It said: *rinnnngggg!*

"Did you hear that?" said Mokey.

"Hooray! The Round Number Ticker said something new," said Gobo.

The Fraggles looked into the water. At the bottom of the Great Pool, they could just make out the Round Number Ticker. But they also saw something else: the reflection of a huge rock, rolling down the slope—heading right for them!

26

Quickly, the Fraggles scattered. They got out of the way just in time. The huge rock rolled into the Great Pool, landing with a tremendous splash. Luckily, nobody was hurt—not even the Round Number Ticker. But everyone was very shaken up.

When the Fraggles caught their breath, Gobo said, "You know, if the Round Number Ticker hadn't gone *rinnnngggg!* just then, we never would have known about that huge rock. The Round Number Ticker saved us!"

"Let's thank it!" said Red.

The Fraggles dived to the bottom of the Great Pool and got the Round Number Ticker.

Gobo dried it off carefully and said, "You really did care about us the whole time! I'm sorry we didn't understand you."

The Round Number Ticker answered: *tick-tick-tick-tick.*

After that, the Fraggles made a special seat for the Round Number Ticker right next to the Great Pool. Whenever they went near it, they would tell it hello and give it a pat.

"That Round Number Ticker may not have too much to say," said Gobo to Mokey, "but it was there when we needed it."

"I know," said Mokey. "And isn't that what friends are for?"

Time Out for Gobo

Can you help Gobo learn how to tell time with the Round Number Ticker? Each clock on this page tells the time of day when Gobo does some special thing. As you read along, point to the clock that matches the time when Gobo does each thing. Here's a hint:

Match the colors of the numbers.

Gobo wakes up at **7** o'clock.

He takes a singing lesson at **10** o'clock.

Lunch is at **12** o'clock noon.

At **3** o'clock, Gobo and Mokey go for a hike.

Gobo takes a bath at **6** o'clock.

Another busy day has ended, and Gobo goes to sleep at **8** o'clock.

Rowlf's Lullaby

"Yaaaaawwwwn! I'm going to sleep," said Rowlf, as he marched off to his bedroom. Today had been a very busy day. "And tomorrow," thought Rowlf, "is going to be even busier. I promised Kermit I'd write a go-to-sleep song. If I don't get some rest, I'll never think of the right notes."

By Jim Lewis   Illustrated by Richard Walz

Rowlf's bed was warm and cozy, with a big puffy pillow and soft fluffy blankets. He settled himself between the covers, gave one more great big yawn, and was off to . . .

PLINK! PLINK! PLINK!

"What?" said Rowlf, sitting up in bed.

It was just the faucet dripping in the sink. "I'll fix that tomorrow," thought Rowlf, "just as soon as I write Kermit's go-to-sleep song. Right now, I'm going to sleep."

Rowlf closed his eyes, put his head on the pillow, and was off to . . .

WHOOO! WHOOO! BONK!

WHOOO! WHOOO! BONK!

"Huh?" said Rowlf, raising himself up on his paws.

It was just the window shutters blowing in the breeze.

"I'll tie those down tomorrow," thought Rowlf, "just as soon as I write Kermit's go-to-sleep song and fix the dripping faucet. But now, I'm going to sleep."

So Rowlf shut his eyes and was quickly off to. . .

YIP! YIP! AH-ROOO!

YIP! YIP! AH-ROOO!

"What's that?!" exclaimed Rowlf, rushing to the window. It was just Rowlf's cousins, Bow and Wow Barkington, out in the alley singing a dog song. Rowlf liked their song, but not so late at night.

"Tomorrow I will ask them not to sing so loud," thought Rowlf, "just as soon as I write Kermit's go-to-sleep song, fix the dripping faucet and tie down the shutters. But right now, I'm going to sleep."

So Rowlf climbed back into bed, pulled up the covers and was almost sound asleep. . .

WEEEE! GEEEE! WEEEE!
GEEEE! WEEEE! GEEEE!

"Who's making that noise?" said Rowlf, tossing off his covers.

From downstairs Rowlf heard Gonzo's voice.

"Sorry, Rowlf! Our All-Mouse Choir has no place else to practice. So I brought them here. I hope it's okay!"

"Sure, Gonzo!" called Rowlf.

"I'll give Gonzo and his All-Mouse Choir a key to my music room," thought Rowlf, "just as soon as I write Kermit's go-to-sleep song, fix the dripping faucet, tie down the shutters, and remind Bow and Wow Barkington not to sing so loud so late at night."

By now it was very late and Rowlf was very tired. But he couldn't fall asleep. He lay in bed and stared at the ceiling.

"Oh, dear," he thought. "If I don't get to sleep, I'll never think of the right notes for Kermit's go-to-sleep song. Which means that I won't". . .

PLINK! PLINK!
"fix the dripping faucet" . . .

WHOOO! WHOOO! BONK! . . .
"tie down the shutters " . . .

YIP! YIP! AH-ROO! . . .
"talk to Bow and Wow Barkington about not singing so loud or". . .

WEEEE! GEEEE! WEEEE! GEEEE! . . .
"give Gonzo and his All-Mouse Choir the key to my
music room."

Now, as everyone knows, some of our best ideas come when
we're about to fall asleep. And sure enough, just as he was
drifting off, Rowlf had one of his best ideas ever.

"I'll make all those noises into music!" he said. And Rowlf
began to sing, to the tune of Brahms' famous lullaby:
"WHOOO! WHOOO! BONK!
WHOOO! WHOOO! BONK!
PLINK! PLINK! PLINK! PLINK! PLINK! PLINK! PLINK!
WEEEE! GEEEE! YIP!
WEEEE! GEEEE! YIP!
AH-ROO! AH-ROO!
WHOOO! WHOOO! BONK! . . ."

It was a perfectly
wonderful go-to-sleep
song. It was so
wonderful, in fact, that
Rowlf fell asleep at the
last BONK.

And there he is,
sound asleep in his
warm, cozy bed. Shhh!
He needs his rest.
Tomorrow is going to
be a very, very busy day.

Fozzie's Not Invited

"Bzzzz, bzzzzz, picnic, bzzz, bzzzz, fun."

Those were the words that drifted on the breeze toward Fozzie as he passed by Kermit's front porch one warm spring morning. Fozzie could see Gonzo and Kermit sitting close together on the porch, laughing and talking.

By Ellen Weiss   *Illustrated by Richard Walz*

Fozzie waved as he walked past.

"Hmmm," he said to himself. "Sounds as though maybe there's going to be a picnic. This is great weather for it. I wonder why nobody told me about it."

Farther down the street, Fozzie saw Piggy and Janice saying good-bye to Rowlf in front of the supermarket.

"See you at the picnic!" called Piggy as Rowlf went into the store.

"Hmmmm," said Fozzie to himself. "It seems as if everybody knows about this picnic but me."

As it happened, Fozzie was also on his way to the supermarket. He looked for Rowlf when he got inside, but didn't bump into him until they were in the checkout line

"Hi, there," said Rowlf, smiling.

Fozzie couldn't help looking to see what was in Rowlf's shopping cart. There were rolls, carrot sticks, bananas and oranges, peanut butter and jelly, paper plates, napkins, and juice. Picnic stuff, it looked like to Fozzie.

"So, ah, Rowlf," said Fozzie carefully. "Doing some, er, picnic shopping?"

"Sure am," said Rowlf. "It's going to be a great afternoon."

"Gee," said Fozzie.

"That's terrific."

Could it really be? Were all his friends having a picnic and not inviting him? It was too awful to think about. Fozzie decided not to think about it. Maybe, he hoped, just maybe he'd made some mistake.

His next stop was the drugstore, to buy some toothpaste. Right in the middle of the toothpaste aisle, who should he run into but Piggy, Animal, and Janice.

"Hi," said Fozzie. "Picking up a few things?"

"Fer sure," said Janice." We're buying picnic stuff." She held up a can of bug spray and a bottle of suntan lotion.

"Picnic! Picnic!" yelled Animal.

So it was true. They were all having a picnic, and they weren't inviting him. How could this be happening? He had thought they were all such good friends. Were they mad at him? Had he done something to hurt them? Or, were there lots of things he didn't get invited to?

Fozzie had never felt so hurt in his life.

He walked and walked, hardly seeing what was around him.

Finally, his feet took him to the bus station at the edge of town.

And there, sitting on a bench were Kermit, Gonzo, Piggy, Janice, Animal, and Rowlf. They had two big picnic baskets and a large, red checked tablecloth.

"Fozzie!" cried Kermit "Where have you been, anyway? We thought we were going to miss the bus, waiting for you!"

"Waiting for me?" echoed Fozzie in confusion. "Why were you waiting for me?"

"To go to the picnic, silly," said Piggy.

"But—but you didn't invite me!" said Fozzie.

"Of course we did," said Kermit. "Piggy did." Kermit turned to Piggy. "Didn't you?" he said.

"I thought you said you were going to ask him," she said.

"No, I thought you were going to!" said Kermit.

"And I thought Janice was going to," said Rowlf.

They all looked sheepish.

"I guess we messed up," said Kermit. "We certainly meant to ask you. We would never leave you out on purpose. We're friends!"

Fozzie beamed happily.

"Say, Fozzie," said Rowlf, "how come you didn't say anything to me before when we were talking about the picnic?"

"I was feeling too hurt to ask," said Fozzie. "I guess, if I ever feel left out again, I should say something about it."

"I sure hope you do," said Kermit as the bus pulled up. "But I sure hope it doesn't happen again."

The driver opened the bus door.

"Where to?" he asked them.

"To the country," said Fozzie happily. "My friends and I are going to have a picnic!"